JFICTION
D'Lace
D'Lacey, Chris

The Dragons of Wayward
Crescent

The Dragons of Wayward Crescent

The Dragons of WAYWARD CRESCENT

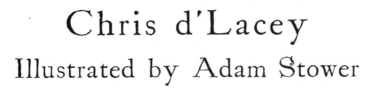

GAUGE

Chris d'Lacey

Illustrated by Adam Stower

ORCHARD BOOKS ◆ NEW YORK
AN IMPRINT OF SCHOLASTIC INC.

Orchard Books is a division of Hachette Children's Books, a
Hachette Livre UK company. All rights reserved. Published by
Orchard Books, an imprint of Scholastic Inc., *Publishers since
1920*, 557 Broadway, New York, New York 10012. ORCHARD BOOKS
and design are registered trademarks of Watts Publishing Group,
Ltd., used under license. SCHOLASTIC and associated logos are
trademarks and/or registered trademarks of Scholastic Inc.

Library of Congress Cataloging-in-Publication Data

D'Lacey, Chris.
  Gauge / by Chris d'Lacey. — 1st U.S. ed.
     p. cm. — (The dragons of Wayward Crescent)
  Summary: When the town council decides to demolish the old
library clock and replace it with a fancy modern one, Lucy and her
mother try to save the historic timepiece — with the help of a dragon.
  ISBN 978-0-545-16831-1 (reinforced bdg. for library use)
  [1. Dragons — Fiction.   2. Clocks and watches — Fiction.
3. Social action — Fiction.   4. England — Fiction.]   I. Title.
  PZ7.D6475Gau 2010
  [Fic] — dc22

                                                    2009029573

10 9 8 7 6 5 4 3 2 1   10 11 12 13 14
              Printed in the U.S.A.   23
              Reinforced Binding for Library Use
              First US edition, January 2010
          This edition's book design by Whitney Lyle

For Chloe and Freya

Chapter One

Burning. Lucy Pennykettle could definitely smell burning. This was not unusual in her house at number 42 Wayward Crescent. Lucy's mother, Liz, made clay dragons for a living, and as everybody knows, dragons breathe fire — well, some of Liz's *special* dragons did, anyway. The fires these dragons breathed were usually quite harmless. They took the form of smoke rings or breathy little *hrrr*s. But this form of burning, the one that was making Lucy's nostrils twitch, seemed to be coming directly from the kitchen. It smelled very much like toast.

"Mom!" she shouted and came charging down the stairs in her pj's and hedgehog-shaped slippers.

Lucy's mom was on the phone in the front room of the house. She was talking away and clearly hadn't heard Lucy or even smelled the burning. Still calling out to her, Lucy hurried on past and into the kitchen. Sure enough, there were two slices of bread toasting on a low flame under the grill of the stove. They were curling at the edges and turning black. Lucy balled her fists. Bravely, she ran to the stove and turned off the gas. But as the jets of blue flame disappeared to nothing there was a gentle *whumph* and the toast itself set on fire.

Lucy gasped and jumped back. "Mom!" she cried again. "There's a fire in the kitchen!" She glanced at the tall green dragon who always sat on top of the fridge. He was a listening dragon, with ears like rose petals. He put on a pair of small round glasses and craned his neck toward the stove.

"Do something!" said Lucy.

The listener sent out an urgent *hrrr*. Within seconds another dragon had zipped into the kitchen to land with a skid and a bump on the counter. His name was Gruffen. He was a guard dragon.

Lucy sighed with relief. "Gruffen, put the fire out."

Gruffen studied the flames. The scaly ridges above his eyes came together in a frown. Strange as it might seem, Gruffen had never actually *seen* a fire before. He was a young dragon, still learning how to puff smoke rings from the back of his throat. He could see there was a problem, but wasn't really sure what the solution might be. The toast made a crackling noise. A flame crept over the griddle.

Lucy gave a little squeal. "Do something!" she repeated.

Gruffen leaped into action: He tapped his claws and consulted his book.

When Liz made one of her special dragons, it was not unusual for them to come with some kind of "magical" object. In Gruffen's case this was a book. A manual of dragon procedures. A directory of things to do in awkward situations. He quickly looked up **"Fire."** There were lots of interesting entries. *Dragon's spark,* said one, *the spirit or life force of the dragon, born from the eternal fire at the center of the Earth.* That made his eye ridges lift. *Source of warming,* said another. *Used in cooking,* said a third. And then there was a rather large entry in red: *WARNING: Fire can be dangerous to humans, but dragons may swallow it without fear (or hiccups).* There was his answer. Gruffen slammed his book shut and flew to the stove.

With one enormous inhale he
sucked the fire toward him and
swallowed it completely. The fire was
immediately put out and the kitchen
was saved. The only problem was
that Gruffen had inhaled so hard

that the toast came flying off the griddle, smashed against his nose, and exploded in a shower of black crumbs. Liz arrived in the kitchen seconds later to find that her normally rosy-cheeked, straw-haired daughter was now the color of charcoal.

"Oh dear," said Liz, waving a hand beneath her nose. "Maybe we'd better have cereal for breakfast instead today."

"That's not funny," Lucy said sourly. "I called you twice."

"Henry Bacon called," Liz explained, taking a damp cloth to Lucy's face. "I didn't expect him to be on the phone so long, but you know what he's like."

Lucy grunted like a farmyard pig. Henry Bacon, the Pennykettles' grumpy next-door neighbor, was always causing problems. "What did he want?"

"He called to say that the town council is planning to demolish the library clock."

"What for?"

"Because it's old and doesn't work very well."

"It tells the wrong time," Lucy agreed. "And it clunks instead of chimes."

"Then it should be fixed, not

demolished," Liz said. "That clock is part of the town's history. People would miss it. It's not right to take it down."

Lucy shrugged. "What about the ghost?"

Her mother laughed. "Ghost? What ghost?"

On the counter, Gruffen looked up "**Ghost.**" *Strange spectral creatures*, his book informed him. *Often found at a place of great unhappiness.*

"Miss Baxter says it's haunted," Lucy sniffed. Miss Baxter, Lucy's teacher, knew about these things. She often went on visits to huge homes. She claimed she had once seen the ghost of Henry VIII eating a chicken drumstick in a closet. Miss Baxter, it had to be said, was slightly strange.

Liz walked away, shaking her bright red hair. "The only thing that haunts that clock tower is pigeons."

"Dead pigeons?" said Lucy, frightened, her mind dizzy with images of ghostly birds going "coo" (or would it be "woo" if they were ghosts?) while flying through walls.

"Just pigeons," said her mom. She

looked out of the window and thought for a second. "It would be such a shame to see that clock go. I feel like I should be doing more to save it. . . ."

Lucy glanced up and the dragons looked at each other. They all knew what was in Liz's mind. Whenever Lucy's mom became concerned about something, she only followed one course of action. She made a new dragon.

A *special* one.

Chapter Two

Liz started it later that night when Lucy had gone to bed.

Along the hallway next door to Lucy's bedroom was a small rectangular room that Liz called her pottery studio, although its nickname was the Dragons' Den.

At the end of the window was a sturdy wooden bench, where Liz kept her paintbrushes and potter's wheel and all the things she needed for making dragons. The two longer walls were taken up with shelves, where there stood a large number of completed dragons. Most of these were in storage, waiting to be sold at the market in town, though some were treasured ornaments and some . . . well, some, like Gruffen, could spread their wings and move around if they wanted to.

In appearance, the Pennykettle dragons looked the same. Their glaze was a mid- to bottle-green color, with

occasional streaks of blue or tur-
quoise. And they all had spiky wings
and curving tails and oval-shaped
eyes and trumpet-like noses. Liz
enjoyed sculpting them in different
poses. She had dancing dragons,
sports dragons, baby dragons break-
ing out of their eggs — dragons in
all sorts of appealing poses. But
those dragons that were special
appeared without conscious effort, as
though they had simply popped out
of Liz's dreams. This is how it was
with the dragon that came to be
known as Gauge.

Lucy Pennykettle, like her mom,
had an instinct for the birth of a

special dragon. As Liz was twisting the wheel back and forth, carefully admiring her latest creation, Lucy slipped into the Den.

"You're supposed to be in bed," said her mom.

Lucy ignored her and came to stand by the worktable. She peered at the dragon. "It's a 'he,'" she said, gently stroking his "topknot" — the little spike that rose like a fin from the top of a dragon's head. "What does he do?"

"I don't know," Liz replied. "But he's definitely special. I was just daydreaming and there he was."

"He's got a paw missing." Lucy pointed to the dragon's left arm. The paw at the end of it seemed to be only half there. But as the moonlight shifted across the window she now saw that he was wearing a kind of vest and was dipping his paw into a shallow pocket. "He's got something,"

she said. Her eyes glowed with excitement.

Her mother hummed in acknowledgment. "Well, if you want to know what it is, you'd better hurry off downstairs."

Lucy was gone in a flash. She knew exactly what her mother meant. In the freezer compartment of the fridge was a small plastic box with a pale blue lid. Inside the box was, of all things, a snowball. Liz had kept it since she was a girl. There were many secrets surrounding this nugget of ice, and even Lucy didn't know all of them. But the snow was what brought her mother's dragons to life. That was all that mattered to Lucy.

She scooted upstairs and handed the box over. Liz opened the lid, letting a bit of condensation escape. The snowball glistened in the moonlight. Lucy held her breath as her mother broke off the tiniest chunk and let it rest on the new

dragon's snout. Immediately, it melted inside his nostrils.

"There, the kilning process is started," said Liz. Then she turned the dragon until he was facing a tall, elegant female dragon who sat alone on a shelf just behind the bench. Her name was Guinevere. Liz whispered something to her in the ancient language of dragontongue. Guinevere's eyes slid open.

Lucy's shoulders bristled with excitement. She had always wanted to know what happened next, but the most she ever saw was a violet light shining out of Guinevere's eyes. That was all she saw this time as well. The light shone over the new dragon's body, creating what looked like a slight halo of fire around him.

Her mother turned Lucy away then, saying, "Come on. Guinevere will hurr when he's ready. Oh, by the way, while you were downstairs a name came to me."

"Really?" said Lucy. This was quite unusual. Dragons weren't usually named until they were active.

"I think he's got a watch in his pocket," said Liz, "because the name I thought of was Gauge."

Lucy didn't look impressed. "Gauge?" she queried.

"It's a word that means 'to measure.'"

"What's he going to measure with a watch?"

"Time, I suppose."

Lucy's shoulders sank. "That's boring," she muttered.

But as usual, where special dragons were concerned, she was in for a few surprises.

Chapter Three

It was another two days before Guinevere signaled to the listening dragon and he, in turn, signaled to Liz to say that Gauge was ready. Liz was in the kitchen at the time, having a cup of tea with Mr. Bacon. Henry did not believe in dragons. So he did not hear the listener's *hrrr*, but was close enough to feel a warm draft in his left ear, which prompted him to ask if Mrs. P., as he called Liz, had left a burner on.

She said she had not and it was just a dragon breathing. That made Henry frown and caused Lucy to stifle a laugh. They enjoyed teasing Henry, though care was needed when a new dragon was in the house. Young special dragons had to be taught that they needed to act like solid clay figures when strangers were near.

While Lucy dashed upstairs to see what was happening, Liz continued chatting to Henry. "Go on. You were talking about the plans to get rid of the library clock. Why can't the council just fix it?"

"Too costly," said Henry, wiggling a finger around in his hairy ear.

"It's surely cheaper than knocking it down and installing a new one?"

Henry shook his head. "Needs a specialist's attention. Old workings. Cranky. Cheaper to rip it out and put in a digital clock."

Liz sighed in dismay. "We can't have flashing neon bulbs in the middle of an old market town. It's completely out of character. I will protest. And so will others."

But to her further dismay, Henry leaned forward and said, "Too late, Mrs. P. Word has it the motion has already been passed. Decided behind closed doors." He beat his fist down lightly on the table, enough to make his teacup rattle against its saucer.

Liz folded her arms (never a good sign) and let out a little puff of disgust. "Well, the ghost won't like it!" she blurted.

"Ghost?" said Henry, closing one eye.

Liz tapped her foot. Goodness, she thought, she had turned into Lucy in the space of a few seconds. "The clock tower is . . . haunted," she said.

"Ridiculous!" cried Henry, slapping his thigh. "Worked in that library twenty years, Mrs. P. Never seen a ghost or heard the slightest hint of wailing — apart from the time Miss Hickinbottom dropped a large encyclopedia on her toe."

"Well, if I were the town council, I'd be careful," said Liz. "You shouldn't mess around with the supernatural."

Henry drummed his fingers. "No such thing as the supernatural," he declared, just as a dragon fluttered into the kitchen and landed on the three long hairs of his nearly bald head. "What the . . . ?" he cried. He jumped in his chair and felt for the spot. But by then, Gauge had fluttered onto the top of the fridge to say hello to the listener.

"Mom, I couldn't control him!" Lucy cried, appearing, out of breath, at the kitchen door.

"What hit me?" said Henry, still rubbing his head and starting to look around.

Liz sighed heavily and snapped her fingers to get Henry's attention. As their eyes met, Liz's gaze became a strange hypnotic stare, and the color of her eyes turned from green to violet. "Go home, Henry. Have a nice sleep," she said.

A dizzy look spread across Henry's face. He rose up like a robot and was gone.

"Sorry," Lucy said sheepishly to her mom.

"It's all right," Liz said, letting her eyes return to green. "Henry won't remember a thing." She glanced at the meeting taking place on top of the fridge. She spoke in dragontongue to Gauge, who fluttered to her open hand. "You need to learn the house rules — and quickly."

Gauge flicked his tail and looked at her with wide, admiring eyes. He dipped his hand into his waistcoat pocket and, just as Liz had predicted, brought out a watch. He gave a gentle questioning *hrrr*.

"You want to know *how* quickly?" Liz translated.

Gauge gave a nod.

Liz glanced through the window. "By the time it gets dark?" she suggested, wondering if he would even understand the concept of sunrises and sunsets at his young age. Though you could never tell with dragons. Sometimes, they could do or know extraordinary things. And so it was with Gauge.

He flipped open his watch and stared at its display. Liz and Lucy leaned forward to share a look.

"That's not a watch," said Lucy. For there were no hands or numbers or a date window to see. Instead, they glimpsed what appeared to be a miniature solar system of planets whirling around one another. And possibly some stars. All deeply reflected in Gauge's eyes.

Liz nodded in astonishment. "I

think that's more than a watch," she said. "I think it's a kind of tuning device."

"What?" said Lucy. She was now completely confused.

"I think this dragon is in touch with the universe," Liz said.

And to answer Liz's question, Gauge said that nightfall was

predicted in eight Earth hours, twelve Earth minutes, and ten Earth seconds — though he wasn't quite sure, yet, what that meant. He flipped the watch shut.

"He's weird," said Lucy. "What use is a dragon that times things?"

"I don't know," said Liz, but her thoughts, like the planets in Gauge's watch, were steadily whirring. And though she couldn't see how Gauge could possibly help with it yet, those thoughts kept returning to the problem of saving the library clock.

Chapter Four

In the meantime, however, Lucy's question, "What use is a dragon that times things?" was quickly answered. It soon became apparent that Gauge had a built-in desire to learn how to measure everything, particularly anything to do with time. He first demonstrated this when he caught sight of the clock on the wall above the door of the kitchen. It was quite an ordinary clock, as clocks go, but the motion of the second hand ticking around seemed to throw the special dragon into a frenzy of delight. He flew out of Liz's hands and hovered in front of it. He tapped the plastic casing. The clock ticked on. Gauge consulted his watch, as if he was using it as a device to check the clock's accuracy. Then something extraordinary happened. Gauge put his watch away and hurred at the clock. Suddenly, its two large hands began to spin, faster and faster, until they were just a blur of black lines. At the same time, Gauge was copying the movements with his paws. This continued until the clock hands had spun all the way back to the correct time again. Then it ticked on as if nothing had happened.

Gauge blew a smoke ring and fluttered down onto the kitchen table.

"Mom, what did he just do?" asked Lucy.

Liz ran a finger down the scales on Gauge's spine, a tickling process all the dragons loved. "I think he just learned to tell the time," she said. "Earth time, at least."

"What other time is there?" Lucy asked, wrinkling her nose. She was finding this dragon very puzzling.

Liz just smiled and said, "What time is it, Gauge?"

Gauge stretched his arms and held his paws at the 11:27 position. Perfect, according to the clock.

"Do three o'clock," said Lucy, just to test him.

His paws swept into the correct places.

"Quarter to seven?"

He was spot-on again.

"Midnight?"

He clapped his paws together, high above his head.

Lucy made a slight *hmph*. She put her hands behind her back and leaned forward until her nose was almost touching Gauge's snout. "Try . . . my bedtime." She grinned.

Gauge frowned and looked side-ways at Liz.

"That's not fair. He can't know

that," said Liz. She paused a moment and tapped her chin. "Lucy's bedtime is eight thirty at night, Gauge. And she's supposed to be asleep no later than nine."

The little dragon sat up and blinked his eyes twice, making a sound like a cash register.

"Why did he do that?" asked Lucy. "Why did he make that noise when he blinked?"

"I can't imagine," Liz said, trying to stop a crafty smile from showing on her face. "Maybe we'll find out later. Now, what are we going to do about the library clock?"

"Who cares about the silly library clock?"

"I do. I think we should stage a protest."

Lucy didn't like the sound of that. At school, Miss Baxter had once told the class about a group of women who had chained themselves to railings because they weren't allowed to vote in elections. When Lucy had asked, "What happened if you wanted to go to the bathroom?" Miss Baxter replied, "You just *went* where you were, my dear!" It was all part of the protest, apparently.

"I don't want to be chained to a railing," said Lucy. What if a fly were to land on her nose? Or squirrels hopped up and nipped her ankles? There were lots of squirrels in the gardens next to the library. Besides, if her friends saw her, they would laugh.

"Don't be silly," Liz said. "You can hand out flyers while I walk up and down the library sidewalk with a sign."

"It's Sunday," Lucy pointed out. "No one will be there, Mom. Anyway, it's raining."

Lucy was right about that. The sky had turned a dull gray color and raindrops were already spattering the windows.

"More time for us to prepare, then," Liz said.

"Time?" Gauge said, pricking his ears.

"Thirteen o'clock," said Lucy.

"Don't tease him," Liz warned her. "You might regret it."

"How?" Lucy snorted. "I'm not frightened of a dragon who *times* things."

* * *

But Liz was right. Later, Lucy did come to regret her words. As the day crept into evening and the time approached eight thirty, Lucy was sitting in the living room reading a book when Gauge jumped onto her knee and hurred.

"What?" she asked.

He pointed to the ceiling.

"It's your bedtime," Liz muttered. "Thank you, Gauge."

"I haven't finished my story," Lucy said grumpily. She lifted her book again.

Gauge spiked her gently with his tail.

"Ow!" she protested.

"Bedtime," her mother repeated. She hadn't even looked up from the book she was reading. "Go on. I'll be up shortly to tuck you in. And don't forget to brush your teeth."

Lucy shut her book and stomped upstairs.

When the door had closed Liz said to Gauge, "Teeth brushing — two whole minutes."

Gauge blinked and made the cash register sound. He flew upstairs.

He kept Lucy at the sink until the toothpaste was practically foaming from her mouth. He made certain that she brushed, flossed, and rinsed — all of which took precisely two minutes. Then, at nine on the dot, he switched off her light.

At eight the next morning, he woke her with a *hrrr* inside her left ear. At breakfast, he timed the perfect boiled egg (three minutes and fifty-eight seconds), and made Lucy chew every mouthful of cornflakes thirty-two times, so that she would not suffer indigestion.

It was starting to drive her crazy. "Mom, he's getting on my nerves," she said. "I'm going to chain myself to . . . the toilet if he doesn't stop timing me!"

"He's just doing his job," Liz said. "There, what do you think about that?" She turned around a large sheet of paper. On it was a rhyme:

TICK TOCK, TICK TOCK, SAVE THE SCRUBBLEY LIBRARY CLOCK!

45

IF YOU CARE ABOUT OUR TOWN,
JOIN OUR PROTEST!
JOIN IT NOW!

"Yeah, Mom. Really impressive."

"I thought so, too." Liz beamed. "I bet lots of people will join in."

Lucy chewed her cornflakes. Thirty, thirty-one, thirty-two. She took another spoonful. "Then what?"

Liz's green eyes sparkled with a hint of mischief. "When we've got enough people on our side, we'll take over the library, sit on the floor, and lock ourselves in."

"*What?*" Lucy dropped her spoon. A spot of milk landed on Gauge's

snout. He licked it off with one quick sweep of his tongue.

"Mom, have you gone crazy?"

"It's important to protect the town's traditions, Lucy."

"But we'll be *arrested*! We'll be in the papers!"

"Mmm, with any luck," Liz said brightly. "We'll probably make the front page. Goodness, I'd better go and brush my hair!"

Chapter Five

Lucy could not believe it. She was going to be a criminal — at the age of nine! She had been to a police station once before, when she was four and had lost her bike. The police had been very kind, and had given her a lollipop because she had cried.

But if her mother's plans to storm the town library were successful, the police would be sure to take a much harsher view. She would be put into a prison cell and made to eat oatmeal. Oatmeal! Yuck! It was horrible stuff. And they would take her photograph — from her worst side! And make her give inky fingerprints. They might even march her off to court. She would have to see a judge! It was hopeless. She might be sent to prison for years. All for the sake of a silly clock!

She frowned at Gauge. He was sitting in front of her on her bedroom table, timing her doing her homework. She was supposed to spend half an hour on her school cooking project. This week it was a recipe for soup. Lucy had come up with the idea of bacon soup, because she blamed Mr. Bacon for telling her mother about the library clock in the first place. The project wasn't going well. She looked at Miss Baxter's notes. *Your soup should make the taste buds tingle while still being nutritious. Do not be afraid to experiment with your ingredients!* So far, Lucy's list of ingredients were water and bacon. It didn't sound very tingling at all.

"How long?" she said to Gauge.

"One more Earth minute," he hurred. He glanced at what she'd written. He didn't look impressed.

Lucy wrote the words "stock cubes" underneath "bacon." According to her mother, chicken stock cubes were good with everything. Ice cream? she wondered. Would they work with milky desserts?

She sighed. This was ridiculous. Her life was now a series of silly thoughts. But as she glanced at Gauge again and saw the willingness to be helpful in his violet eyes (a quality that every special dragon possessed), suddenly an idea came to her.

"Can you *fix* clocks?" she asked.

Gauge tilted his head.

"You know, can you take them apart and put them back together and make them, y'know, tick correctly again? Or bong?"

Gauge tapped his foot. He wasn't sure, he said — especially about the bonging. He wasn't meant to be a fixing dragon.

"But you could *try*," said Lucy. "If I took you to the clock tower, you might be able to make it chime correctly again. Then we wouldn't have to do the protest, would we?"

Before Gauge could answer, the

doorbell rang, and Liz let Henry Bacon into the house. Lucy heard Henry saying that Liz might be interested to know that tomorrow afternoon, in the library, a Mr. Trustable of the Town Council was going to present the new plans for the improved clock tower, and would she like to attend? Liz said she would *definitely* like to attend. Lucy gulped. She felt the end of her pencil snap. She knew exactly what her mother was thinking.

Then Henry said, "On the subject of clocks, Mrs. P., can you help with this? Trying to get a battery into my pocket watch. Very tricky. Fingers a bit shaky."

"Oh, Lucy's the expert at that kind of thing," Liz said.

She had hardly called upstairs before Lucy was in the kitchen, panting, "I'll do it!" She shot back up with the watch and the battery before Liz had had time to switch the kettle on.

"There," she said to Gauge, putting it at his feet. "Practice on that."

Gauge looked at it doubtfully. It was a beautiful old watch. It had a cream-colored face with golden numerals. He didn't want to break it, he said.

Lucy turned the watch over. Henry had already removed the back plate and flipped the old battery out of its

54

housing. "Just look," she said. "It works off one of these." She broke open the new battery packet. "I bet the library clock just has a bigger battery, that's all. Here." She handed it to him.

Gauge took it between his paws. The battery immediately began to crackle and an arc of blue light sparked between his ear tips. A puff of smoke came out of his nostrils. The end of his tail began to jiggle.

"Are you all right?" asked Lucy.

Gauge nodded and put the battery down. Gwendolen, Lucy's own special dragon, who sat in the shadow of her bedside lamp, asked if she might try holding it. Lucy said no and tapped the watch again.

Gauge peered at the inside of the watch. He could see two metal wheels with zigzagging teeth all around their edges. The wheels were meshed together. Neither wheel was moving, but it was obvious to Gauge that they would if this energy cell that Lucy called a battery was able to power them. He drummed his claws. He felt sure there were more workings underneath the wheels and pointed to another circle of metal that had a straight groove cut across it. There were lots of those,

of different sizes, all over the back of
the watch.

"They're called screws," said Lucy.
"If you turn them, they sort of open."

Gauge's eyes lit up in wonder.
This was a far more interesting
timing machine than the clock in the
kitchen. He pointed to the screws

again, one by one, and to his
amazement they began to unwind
by themselves.

"Wow, that's cool," gasped Lucy.

Now Gauge grew bolder still. As the screws fell out of their holes, he flipped aside the covering they'd been holding in place to reveal a whole assembly of wheels and cogs and levers and springs.

Before long, it was all in pieces on Lucy's table.

"Lucy, how are you doing with that watch?"

Suddenly, Liz's voice came drifting up the stairs.

"Nearly done!" Lucy called back. But she was nervous now. "Um, you *can* put it back together, can't you?" she asked.

Gauge asked if he could he have a few more Earth minutes to study it.

"No," hissed Lucy. "Stick it all back. Now!"

Gauge frowned in dismay and quickly did as he'd been told.

As soon as the back plate went on, Lucy hurried downstairs and handed the watch to Mr. Bacon.

"Thank you, child," he said. His eyebrows knotted. "Hmm, doesn't appear to be going." He shook it and held it to his ear and looked again. "Dead as a doughnut."

Lucy's cheeks began to flush.

"Must be another dead battery," said Liz.

Mr. Bacon sniffed. "Did put the right one in, didn't you, child?"

"Yes!" snapped Lucy, though she remembered the sparks around Gauge's ears and wondered if he may have drained its power.

Just then, Gauge fluttered into the kitchen and landed on the fridge top. This time he turned solid as Henry looked around.

Liz didn't even glance at him. But Lucy did. As her mother saw Henry to the door, Lucy gritted her teeth and scowled.

Gauge was holding a watch wheel in his right paw.

Chapter Six

After school the following day, the gray skies produced a fine drizzle over the town. It would be enough, Lucy hoped, to put her mother off any silly ideas about marching up and down outside the library. But Liz was determined. She made Lucy put on her hooded yellow raincoat. Then she drove them both into town.

The protest sign was by now taped onto a stiff piece of cardboard, which in turn had been tacked, not very securely, to a long wooden stick. Liz rested it against her shoulder and proudly marched the short distance from the parking lot to the sidewalk, chanting her rhyme loudly for all of the town to hear.

Lucy didn't know where to look. But she did her job, handing out the flyers her mother had prepared, and was surprised to hear people clapping and saying, "Good for you!" This brought her some cheer. Hopefully it meant they would at least have some visitors when they were hauled off to jail.

If Lucy had expected the sidewalk to be deserted, she was wrong. A large crowd had gathered by the library doors. They cheered as Liz marched down the sidewalk. One of them dashed forward. To Lucy's dismay, she saw it was her teacher, Miss Baxter.

"Excellent work!" Miss Baxter gushed, eyeing Liz's sign. "Hello, Lucy!"

"Hello, Miss Baxter," Lucy muttered from deep within her hood.

"Couldn't have come at a better moment," said Miss Baxter. "We've just heard that Councilman Trustable is going to make a short speech out here — for the cameras!"

"Cameras?!" Lucy pushed back her hood. To her horror, she saw a TV news crew. The camera was already pointing at the crowd of protesters.

"They're from the regional TV news," said Miss Baxter.

"Wonderful," said Liz.

"I'm going home," said Lucy.

"No, no," said Miss Baxter, drawing her forward. "It's very important for

people to see that the children of the town are just as willing to preserve the old clock as the adults are."

"But I'm the only 'children' here!" Lucy wailed.

"Then perhaps they'll interview you!" Miss Baxter said.

Interview? Lucy's cheeks turned as pale as the white library walls.

Just then, a round of booing began. Lucy looked up to see a handsome man in a long, dark overcoat come strolling out of the library. He was waving a hand as though people were really cheering, not booing. Beside him was another man, who looked like some kind of guard.

The handsome man smiled. He

had teeth like a row of white piano keys. He stepped onto a small podium. The TV camera turned toward him.

"Ladies and gentlemen," the man began.

"And children!" cried Miss Baxter, yanking up Lucy's hand.

"And children," he said, with a smug sort of nod. "My name is Roger Trustable, your local elected councilman —"

"I didn't vote for you!" someone shouted.

"And this is Mr. Higson." He gestured to the shorter man, who rolled his beefy shoulders and sniffed. "We are here today to tell you of a wonderful redevelopment plan for your library."

"Save our clock!" Miss Baxter shouted. The crowd cheered. The camera turned toward them again. (Lucy immediately hid her face.)

Roger Trustable raised an important finger. "The hour beckons and time marches on —"

"Not if you have your way," said Henry Bacon. He was standing, arms folded, by the library doors.

"— when progress must be made."

"Boo!" went Liz.

Lucy gritted her teeth. "Mom," she hissed. The camera was squarely on her mom now. Total embarrassment. They were going to be on the news!

Liz would not be stopped. "We don't want progress of the kind you're talking about! We want history! We want our clock restored!"

"Save our clock! Save our clock!" the crowd began to chant.

Councilman Trustable jiggled his tie. "Our reports indicate that the existing clock cannot be repaired —"

"You're just too cheap to spend money on it, that's all!" Miss Baxter shouted.

The councilman laughed. "If you look at our record over the past two years, madam, you'll see that we've been —"

"Playing the same one!" a heckler shouted.

Lucy did not understand this remark, but it caused a great ripple of laughter all the same. She looked at Councilman Trustable. His cheeks had flushed. He seemed a little annoyed.

"Perhaps if you were to come into the library and view the Council's plans?" he suggested.

"Oh, we will!" said Liz. And she thrust her stick forward so hard that the cardboard sign came off and struck Councilman Trustable in the chest.

The crowd cheered and surged toward the library doors. Lucy squirmed. The dreaded "sit-in" had begun. Worse still, she could see a police car pulling up on the street. All the protesters were now heading for the library, leaving just her, Henry Bacon, the film crew, Councilman Trustable, and his guard, Mr. Higson, behind. This was it. Her life of crime had begun.

The councilman stepped down off his podium. His expression was very harsh. He waved the camera away then whispered something snappy to Mr. Higson. Mr. Higson gave a rude nod and went into the library. He brushed hard past Lucy's shoulder, spinning her around. She turned to find herself in the eye of the camera.

"Want to say something, kid?"

The reporter, a young woman with messy hair and very tight blue jeans, thrust a microphone under Lucy's nose.

Lucy gulped. Two burly policemen strolled past, behind her. In about one minute from now, they would probably come the other way, carrying her mother kicking and screaming to their waiting car.

"Anything?" the reporter asked.

Lucy dipped her hand into her deep coat pocket. She brought out

Gauge and showed him to the camera. It was time she put her own plans into action. "Dragons rule," she said, and dashed into the library.

Chapter Seven

Lucy couldn't believe her eyes. She had never seen the library so full before — not even on Wildest Read Day, when a famous explorer had brought in a snake. The crowd of protesters had swarmed into the gaps between the bookshelves. They were all sitting cross-legged on the floor. All except two: her mother and Miss Baxter. They were standing beside a display board in the local history section. The two policemen and Henry Bacon were making their way toward them.

"Now, ladies —" one of the policemen began.

"This is a peaceful protest!" said Miss Baxter, wagging a finger as if he was her pupil.

"Not from where we're standing," the second policeman said. "This is public disorder. If you don't clear the library, we'll have to arrest you."

"Unless they all take out a book,"

whispered Henry, who was never one to miss an opportunity for a loan.

The policeman waved him aside.

"Boo!" went the crowd. "Save our clock!"

"At least hear us out," Liz said boldly. "We're here to demonstrate how much the people of this town are against these plans." She pointed to the board, where there were some drawings of Councilman Trustable's proposed new clock.

The first policeman sighed. "Between you and me, madam, I don't care for them, either, but invading the library is not the way to get them stopped."

Miss Baxter promptly sat down.

To Lucy's horror, she saw her mother sit down as well.

That was it. Lucy knew that unless she acted, all hope was lost. She hurried to the main library desk. The librarians who normally issued the books had deserted it to watch the hilarious events. Lucy slipped behind it and went to the door that led to the clock tower above. To her surprise, it was open. She peeped inside. It was dark and slightly musty, but she could see a bit of yellow light where the stairs wound upward. A chilly breeze whistled down the old stone steps. Lucy jumped back. She didn't like the dark — or the thought of ghosts.

But the thought of going to prison was even worse. She glanced over her shoulder. The policemen were trying to drag Miss Baxter away. Unbelievably, she had stolen their handcuffs and chained herself to a library cart!

Checking to see that no one was watching, Lucy whispered urgently to Gauge. "Fly up there and see if you can fix the clock. If you can make it bong correctly, that will be enough."

Gauge twitched his nose. He wasn't sure about this. He'd had words with Gruffen before they came out, and Gruffen's book had clearly stated that Pennykettle dragons were not to be let loose in human society unless Liz said so. But on this occasion, he didn't have much choice.

"Go!" Lucy hissed, and threw him up the stairs.

He fluttered around the curving walls, up toward the light. In a matter of minutes he had settled on a dusty wooden platform that was built around the workings of the ancient clock. Its cogs and wheels were huge compared to those in Mr. Bacon's watch. Gauge looked on in fascination as they ground slowly around, making a lovely, deep tock every time one of the wheel teeth engaged.

High above, a pigeon cooed. The clock groaned and gave a dull sort of clunk. Gauge knew it was trying to chime. But something was preventing it. Something unnatural. It was just as if the clock had been hurt in some way. He flew forward to investigate

and landed on a rail beside the main
housing. As he did he heard a footstep.
Instantly, he turned himself solid.

From the far side of the platform a
figure appeared. It was Mr. Higson,
Councilman Trustable's assistant.
Gauge recognized him because he'd
watched all the commotion outside
through a hole in Lucy's pocket. Mr.
Higson was carrying a long piece of

wood. He kept jabbing it at the clock, trying to wedge it between the wheels. It seemed to Gauge that the man was trying to break the clock or stop it from working. That made him very angry indeed. He was wondering if he should risk scorching Mr. Higson's ear when a foggy voice said, "Oh no, sir. That won't do the job at all."

Gauge rolled his eyes. From out of nowhere, another figure had appeared. He was very old and had no hair, apart from two bushy growths on either cheek. He was wearing a vest, which had watch chains looping out of both pockets. Gauge smiled. His angry mood lifted. Here was a man who cared about time.

Mr. Higson whipped around in surprise. "What the . . . ? Where did you come from?"

"Ah, that is a difficult question," said the figure. "I seem to live here permanently now, if that's any help."

"Who are you?"

"I am Sir Rufus Trenchcombe, Clockmaker to the Crown."

Mr. Higson shook his head in confusion. "Are you the, uh, keeper of this clock or something?"

Sir Rufus's chest seemed to swell with pride. "Indeed, one could say so. Do you have an interest in timepieces, sir? Were you seeking to release the stuck counter sprocket by striking it with your plank?"

Mr. Higson clicked his tongue. "I was sent here to, uh, service it, yeah. This, um, counter sprocket. Is that what's wrong with it?"

"Indeed so! Faulty these three years past."

Mr. Higson lifted his piece of wood. "So if that broke, then . . . ?"

"It would need a vast repair. But the part is sturdy. The king's cannon would surely struggle to break it. 'Tis made from the finest metals. A greater problem lies with the pendulum arm."

Mr. Higson gave an interested nod. "And where's that?"

"Why, there," said Sir Rufus. In a flash, he seemed to disappear and reappear instantly on the other side of Gauge. He pointed to a long piece of rope that dangled down into the depths of the tower. "The balancing weight is missing. If this were adjusted and the counter sprocket oiled, my clock would run appropriately and the chime would be restored."

"Oh, would it?" Mr. Higson grunted. He sounded disappointed.

Until Sir Rufus added, "Of course, if the weight is far wrong, then the mechanism will altogether stop."

Mr. Higson narrowed his eyes. He noticed Gauge balancing on the rail. Though he was clearly confused and

wondering
why a clay dragon
was in the tower,
he nevertheless
snatched Gauge
up. "How about
this for a weight?" He tossed Gauge
loosely in his hand.

"A most unlikely prospect," said
Sir Rufus.

The man gave a villainous smile.
"Let's try it."

Before Sir Rufus could argue, Mr.
Higson had pulled up the rope, tied
Gauge to the end of it, and thrown
him down the tower shaft, into the
darkness. The old clock ground to a
weary halt.

Sir Rufus made a strange kind of wailing sound. "Treachery!" he cried. He stretched out a hand as if to rescue Gauge, but his hand passed straight through the rope.

"Aaaah, you're a ghost!" Mr. Higson cried. And with a gurgling scream he fled down the stairs, leaving the clock in silence and Gauge still dangling somewhere in the darkness. . . .

Chapter Eight

Until that point, the policemen had
been struggling to clear the library.
But things were about to change.
As Councilman Trustable's assistant
burst through the door crying, "A
ghost! Help! There's a ghost in the
tower," half the protesters leaped to

their feet. No one needed to be convinced of Mr. Higson's sincerity. His hair was as stiff as a row of staples and his face as white as a Ping-Pong ball. He ran for the glass doors, hit the pane that didn't open automatically, and almost knocked himself out.

"Ghost?" someone asked.

Henry Bacon helpfully put in, "Rumor has it the spirit of Sir Rufus Trenchcombe roams the tower. Utter nonsense, of course."

"You're the librarian. Go and look!" someone cried.

Henry glanced uncomfortably at the stairway. "Not in my job description."

Just then, the library clock gave a deep and resounding bong. Then another. And another. And another. And after a few seconds' gap, another.

"The ghost is angry," someone suggested nervously.

But Lucy thought she could hear a joyous wail floating down the stairs. A ghostly breeze whooshed through the library. People screamed and ran for the street. To Lucy's relief, the policeman who'd been escorting her mother to the door buckled at the knees and promptly fainted.

Lucy saw her chance. She tugged her mom's sleeve and whispered, "Mom, I let Gauge go up there."

Liz rolled her eyes. "Then you'd better go and see what he's up to," she hissed.

Lucy ran toward the tower door. "It's all right, I'm not afraid of ghosts," she shouted. And up the steps she pounded. Not, of course, expecting to encounter Sir Rufus Trenchcombe at the top.

She stopped on the platform, too scared to even shake. The clock bonged again, almost deafening her. "Ah, child," said Sir Rufus. "Can you free the spirit caught on the rope?" He pointed a wispy finger.

Lucy glanced sideways and saw the pendulum rope swinging. Suddenly, Gauge appeared. His wings were beating very hard. He was trying to escape from the shaft, but the heavy rope was making it hard for him to fly. With an exhausted *hrrr*, he fell back into the darkness. The clock responded with another loud bong.

Lucy ran to his aid. She grabbed the rope and pulled it up to the

platform rail. Her nimble fingers quickly released the young dragon. "Are you all right?" she asked.

Gauge shook a cobweb off his tail and nodded. He frowned and turned his head toward the clock. Before Lucy could ask what he was doing, he had flown to the housing and was hurring deeply on one of the big wheels. To her surprise, Lucy saw that a patch of gooey gunk around the wheel was suddenly flowing like oil. The clock gave a heave and the wheel moved freely.

Sir Rufus Trenchcombe whooped with joy. "The counter sprocket! The dragon creature has released the counter sprocket. Now the clock may run more precisely."

Lucy stepped forward and stubbed her toe against something on the floor. "Ow, what's this?" She picked up a heavy piece of metal.

" 'Tis the weight for the pendulum arm," said Sir Rufus. He pointed to the rope.

"You mean, if I tie this on the end, the clock is fixed?" Lucy asked.

"Almost certainly, child."

So Lucy tied on the weight and let it fall down the shaft. Immediately, the clock gave a sequence of chimes. "It works!" she shouted. "It works! It works!"

Sir Rufus drifted toward the clock's machinery. "Hmm. I fear some adjustment may yet be needed. The warmth of the dragon's breath might have caused some damage to the chime counter."

Gauge gave a *hrrr* that sounded like "Oops." He blew a smoke ring and looked a bit sheepish.

Lucy flapped a hand. "Well, you look after that. I've got to save my mom from going to prison now."

"A noble gesture," Sir Rufus said, bowing. "I am indebted to you, child." He put out a hand and tried to shake Lucy's. It was a bit scary, watching a ghost hand bobbing up and down through your own, but Lucy was brave and didn't even squeak.

She picked up Gauge, said good-bye and hurried down the stairs.

To her relief, her mom was still there, using a book to fan the policeman who had fainted. "Mom," she cried. "Gauge fixed the clock!"

The word quickly spread. Those protesters that were still around shouted "Hooray!"

"What about the ghost?" one of them asked.

Lucy said, "He's happy. And the clock works correctly." As if to prove it, high above them the clock began to bong. The crowd cheered loudly.

"Now we can all go home," said Lucy.

"Just one *second*," a smug voice said. It was Councilman Trustable. He turned his wrist and tapped his watch. "By my watch it's four o'clock precisely." He paused and cupped a hand around his ear. "Your clock has just chimed seven. . . ."

Chapter Nine

The next day, it was in all the papers. The protest. Councilman Trustable's new clock plans. The mystery of the ghost of Sir Rufus Trenchcombe. The strange goings-on with the clock.

Lucy sat, deflated, at the kitchen table, reading one paragraph over again. It said:

Although the Trenchcombe clock appears to be chiming better than it has in years, the sequence is completely wrong. Four o'clock has become seven, eleven o'clock has become three, etc., and the clock refuses to bong nine. An expert has said it would be far too costly to change the part required to correct it. The Town Council is therefore recommending that Councilman Trustable's plans be enforced.

Lucy let her head sink onto her arms. "We've failed," she said.

Liz sighed and glanced at Gauge.

The young dragon looked so sad. "It's no one's fault. We all tried our best. Gauge probably wasn't meant to fix clocks, anyway."

Nevertheless, the dragon let his shoulders droop.

"Look, let's go out for a walk," said Liz. "Around the library gardens. We'll take some bread for the ducks."

Lucy sighed. "Only if Gauge can come, too."

Twenty minutes later they were on their way to the library again. Lucy held Gauge to her chest all the way. As they walked down the sidewalk, the little dragon could hardly bear to look at the clock. But, strangely, as they drew closer, a series of clicks and a few light flashes made him raise his eyes. A large group of people had gathered outside the library again. Most of them were carrying cameras.

"Are they protesters?" Lucy asked her mom.

"No, I think they're tourists," Liz said. "Look, they're all taking photographs of the clock."

The cameras flashed and clicked again.

Lucy pointed to Mr. Bacon, who was making an announcement to some of the people. "Next tour of the tower at noon," he was saying. "Five dollars for the chance to see the ghost of Sir Rufus Trenchcombe . . ."

"Well, I never," Liz said. She chuckled softly. Over to one side of the library she could see Councilman Trustable watching the crowd snapping away. He had a thoughtful look on his face. "I think our clock is saved, Lucy. If it becomes a tourist attraction, the last thing the Council will do is knock it down. It will bring people to the town and make lots of money. It looks like Gauge has succeeded after all." She reached over and tickled his ears.

Hrrr! went the dragon. He flapped a paw.

"Careful," whispered Lucy, "you're supposed to be solid."

"Oh, I think we can forgive him this time," said Liz. And she raised a hand as well and waved at a small, dark window in the tower.

From behind it, Sir Rufus Trenchcombe waved back.

Suddenly, his old clock chimed five times.

Lucy looked at her watch. It was noon, or midday. But from that moment on, lunchtime in town would always be known as "five bongs" — all thanks to a dragon named Gauge.

About the Author

Chris d'Lacey is the acclaimed author of several books for children, including *A Break in the Chain*, The Dragons of Wayward Crescent series, and the *New York Times* and *USA Today* bestselling The Last Dragon Chronicles: *The Fire Within*, *Icefire*, *Fire Star*, and *The Fire Eternal*.

He lives in Leicester, England, with his wife, where he is at work on his next book.

Visit www.icefire.co.uk or www.scholastic.com/kids/lastdragonchronicles to learn more about Chris d'Lacey's books.